For my little bears,
Zoe and Alexandra
—B.H.

For my little dude, Brian
—K.B.

Thanks and admiration
for our colorist, Jo Rioux.

Library of Congress catalog card number: 2014934800
ISBN 978-0-06-228598-0

Book design by Victor Joseph Ochoa
15 16 17 18 19 SCP 10 9 8 7 6 5 4 3 2 1 ❖ First Edition

LAZY BEAR, CRAZY BEAR

by Kevin Bolger   illustrated by Ben Hodson

HARPER

An Imprint of HarperCollinsPublishers

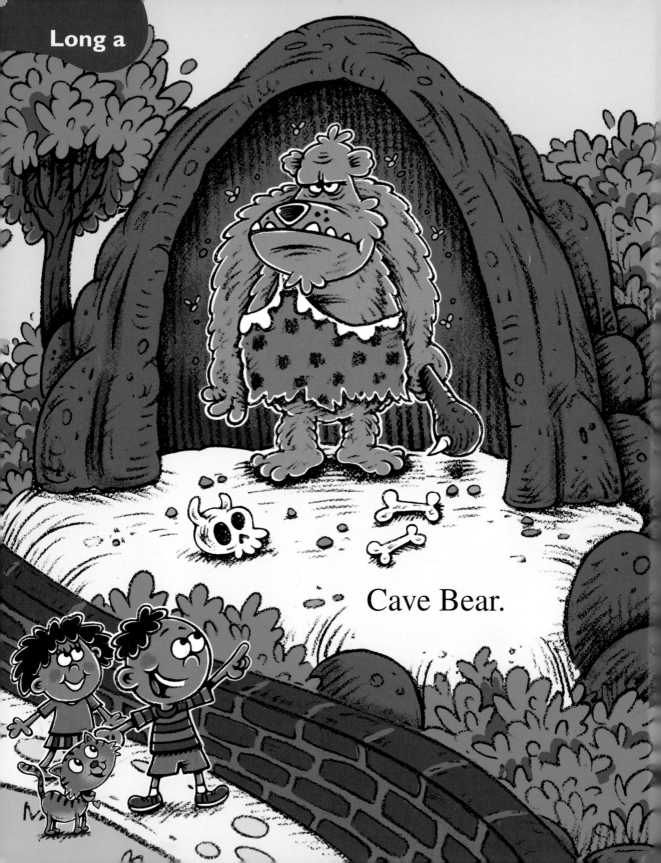

Cave Bear.

Wave Bear.

Lazy Bear.

Crazy Bear.

Bear with plates.

Bear on skates.

Bears at play.

Bears in the way.

Cage of bears.

Page of bears.

Wee Sheep at Sea

Three sheep at the beach.

He sheep. She sheep.

Wee sheep.

Breeze . . .

Wee sheep at sea.

Creature of the deep.

She fears. He screams.

"EEK!"

"Wheeeeeeeee!"

Wee sheep steers back
within reach.

She sheep and He sheep
weep tears of relief.

Next week . . .

Gran's Reading Rules #1:
Long vowels say their own names.

Short a*  **Long a**

snack

snake

Short e **Long e**

Fred

freed

*To learn all about short vowels, read my book, *Gran on a Fan*.

Short i

licks

Long i

likes

Short o

socked

Long o

soaked

Short u

cub

Long u

cube

17

FiVE MiCE oF CRiME...

ride bikes with spikes.

Spy a pie.

Climb up a wire.

Slice with a knife.

19

Slide down the pipe.

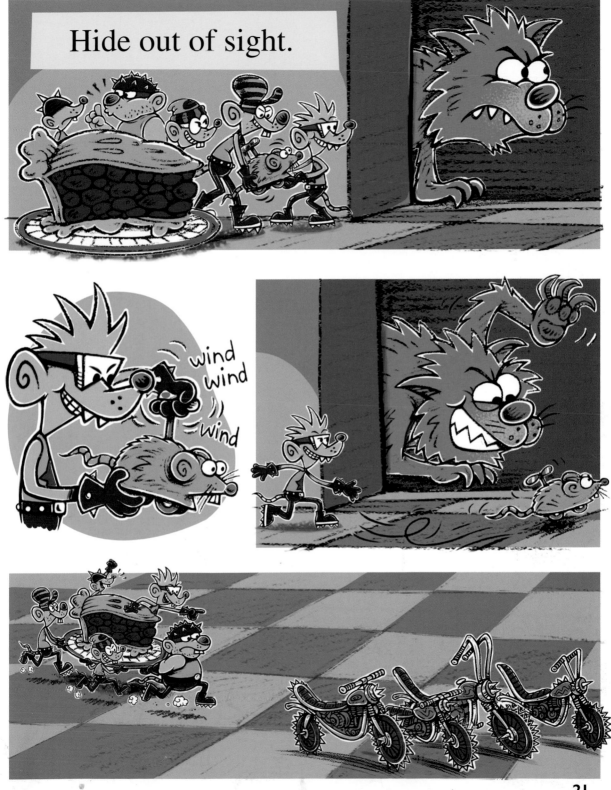

Hide out of sight.

wind wind wind

Fly with their prize.

Try a bite.

Nice!

22

Gran's Reading Rules #2:
A silent **e** at the end of a word makes the vowel in the middle say its own name.

shake

Pete

smile

nose

crude

23

Ghost on the road.

Ghost at the show.

24

Ghost on the shore.

Ghost in the snow.

Ghost in the smoke.

Ghost on the phone.

27

Gran's Reading Rules #3:
When two vowels go walking, the first one does the talking and says its own name.

hair

beak

spies

ROAR!

blue

Dude.

Dude out of fuel.

Dude on a mule.

New dude.

A few dudes.

Huge dude.

Stooge dudes.

Rude dude.

Nude dude.

Cute dude.

Flute dude.

Dude plays a tune.

Dude in the moon.

Gran's Rule Review

Rule #1:

Long vowels say their own names.

cube

Rule #2:

A silent **e** at the end of a word makes
the vowel in the middle say its own name.

smile

Rule #3:

When two vowels go walking, the first one
does the talking and says its own name.

beak

Rule #4: